LOU AND JIGGER

True Love Is Inseparable

By:

Geryn Childress

Chapter 1

Strangely, I can recall my earliest memory as a child - being passed around by the adults in the room. I remember seeing faces and the bright lights of the room. I can hear their voices, one of them saying, "you have to stop her from smoking." I didn't know what that meant at the time, but it's a phrase that's stuck with me ever since.

I was born in Ypsilanti, Michigan, but shortly thereafter my mother decided to throw caution to the wind and left her family. She headed for Shreveport, Louisiana, with my father. This decision didn't sit well with my grandfather, who was a Pentecostal minister at Bethlehem Temple Church of All Nations. Being a man of the cloth, my grandfather had a certain disdain for my father, because he had been married twice before and saw him as a sort of warlock that meant my mother and our family no good.

My mother was the eldest of nine children, and seemed to always disregard tradition in favor of making her own path. She wasn't a very religious woman, but she was definitely spiritual; perhaps this was a result of being raised in a religious home. The main purpose of her leaving Michigan was so her children could have the experience of growing up in the South. There was a certain richness she found in country living, and she believed all children should experience Southern life at least once.

Chapter 2

Shreveport, Louisiana in the early 80's was a totally different world from the rest of America; it was reminiscent of plantation times. People made and sold moonshine, and blacks and whites were still very much segregated and kept to themselves. There weren't many jobs in the South, so my father rummaged through peoples garbage to find things he could fix and sell; a process he called "junkin," which I absolutely loved doing with my father as a child. My parents would also build wells for people who needed a fresh water supply. Sometimes they would travel across town or to a different state to build wells. My mother managed to save up enough money to buy a tattered little home on a small plot of land in Minden, Louisiana. It wasn't much, but to us it was home. My brother and I were often left with a babysitter, who came to be more of a grandmother to us. We called her Mama Rosie. We seemingly spent more time with her than our actual mother during that time. Mama Rosie lived on 10 acres of fertile land. She had a small farm with chickens, pigs, and a beautiful garden that stretched for what seemed like forever. There was an old stone well that sat quietly in back of the garden that was over grown with vines. I loved that well. Looking down the deep dark opening was like looking into space; at least that's what I imagined space to look like, being only five years old. My brother and I would help Mama Rosie tend to her garden as much as we could. She didn't have much, but what she did have she gave to me and my brother, as if we were her own grandchildren. Despite the lack of running water, and having to use an outhouse, growing up in the South was a wonderful experience. One of the main chores me, my brother Ken, Danny Ray and Peaches(Mama Rosie's grandchildren) all took part in was fetching water from the well. I remember sometimes the pail we would lower down into the well would come up with a catfish in it. In the South at that time, they'd put a catfish in a well to help clean the water...Those were some of my best times as a child.

Chapter 3

There were always interesting characters coming by Mama Rosie's house, such as Jimmy the wino, who loved Mama Rosie's moonshine; Squala, a real Native American who would come out of the forest once every few months and sometimes spend the night in the abandoned 1973 Chevelle that was broken down and stood as an adornment on Mama Rosie's property. A host of others would stop by wanting to buy some of Mama Rosie's moonshine or hog head cheese. I remember once Squala bought a bag full of turtle eggs from the forest, and I watched him put the turtle eggs in his mouth and bite down slowly. The little turtles were still alive and moving inside the eggs, and you could hear the "CRUNCH" sound they made. That sound haunts me till this day. Squala was one of the only friends I had as a child. My mother for some reason beyond my comprehension was always fixing my hair up in ponytails so none of the other neighborhood boys wanted to play with me. "We're not playing with that girl!" they would shout. One of my most embarrassing moments was Mama Rosie pulling down my pants and shouting back at the other boys, "Look! He's got the same thing you got down there!" It didn't work, so Squala was all that I had. He couldn't speak English and only made weird grunting noises, but I could always understand what he meant by his hand gestures. My brother was five years older than me, and little brothers aren't fun to have tag along with you, especially when you first arrive in a new environment and you're trying to fit in and make friends yourself. Squala's friends were the trees and plants in the forest, and often I would see him grunting at an old oak tree and bushes in the back of Mama Rosie's property. As a child, it seemed almost as if they were communicating with him in some way. That is something that has stuck with me all these years as well.

Mama Rosie always had interesting stories to tell. One day while sitting on her lap she said, "Boy! Did I ever tell you the story about Lou and Jigger?" "No-ma'am," I replied. She leaned back in her old wicker rocking chair, pulled me a little closer, and began the story.

Chapter 4

Ebe Johnson was just about the meanest ol' bastard you ever wanted to meet, and he died just as wicked as the day he was born.

Luella, his great granddaughter, was a good girl. The eldest of five, mildly attractive, timid, but dedicated. She looked after her brothers and sisters as if they were her own children.

She loved her mama and daddy, though he was just about as mean as old Ebe. She even loved her old grandaddy, mean as he was. She loved them all except when it came to "Jigger."

Jigger was a boy up the road who'd been making eyes at Luella. He was a nice ol' boy, really. She didn't have any marks against him. It's just that Ebe didn't like him. And when Ebe spoke it - it was law.

The Sunday gatherings and chance meetings in the field didn't quell their passion. Soon they were meeting secretly in the barn back of Jiggers. Grandpa Ebe finally caught them. He whipped Louella and almost killed Jigger with the harness straps that hung conveniently on the wall. He told him if he ever set foot in Sumpter again, he'd kill him.

Lou was pregnant once before, but miscarried. The shame she brought on her family and the emptiness she felt with Jigger gone contributed to her losing the only baby she would ever carry.

It was sad that Grandpa Harebell rejoiced at the baby's death, but it was typical of his behavior. On his own deathbed, he cursed his dying, wishing, instead, that, "it was that damned boy!"

Jigger came back bitter and hurt. He had heard of the deaths. Louella could sense his return. And just as they always did, she met him at the barn. Only now, they continued seeing each other. She had only the clothes on her back and the little money she had managed to save. He had healed and come to take her away. Their freedom landed them in Missouri where they were married and lived together in bliss, totally isolated from her family for twenty years, before coming back to seek peace with her father.

Chapter 5

Luella's father was old, but still tough and bitter. His pride and his father's word had gone before him; and forgiving was beneath his dignity. He made peace, only to the extent that he promised not to kill them. But the hate was still there.

Lou and Jigger had brought enough money with them from Missouri to buy a shotgun house and a little piece of land. They didn't need much for just the two of them. Though they hadn't been blessed with any children, they counted the blessings they had and kept loving each other, vowing to live and die this life together.

Jigger worked hard at making his house a home. He was a good man and could fix anything. He spent as much time working on Esau's(his father-in law's) houses as he did his own. Louella baked and cooked for her father. All of this for love and peace's sake, but Esau remained just as callous and insensitive as he had always been. He would sit on the porch and smile wickedly at Jigger laboring relentlessly. Louella's heart would have broken if she had known her father was throwing away every morsel of food she brought into his house.

They lived in a vacuum. His family bore them no grudge, but couldn't take the pressures associating with them, so they kept their distance. Rare visits from them were generally confined to nighttime. Lou and Jigger didn't fault them. They understood. None of her sisters or brothers ever visited them and the children were forbidden to even walk on the side of the road in front of their house. Harebell and Esau's hatred was far reaching and seemed eternal.

One fall, Esau finally got his grips on them both. He had heard about Jigger buying half a hog from an old white man and seized upon this opportunity to get revenge. He loaded his hogs late one night and hauled them over fifteen miles to a friend and swore him to secrecy about how he had gotten them. Early the next morning, he drove his wagon straight to Sheriff Haynes to report his hogs stolen by, none other than, Jigger. He had been around long enough that, like his father, if he said it, it was so.

Jigger was hauled from his house mercilessly; crying and begging, pleading his innocence. Louella was numbed by it all. "Daddy, tell them the truth. Tell them, Daddy," she pleaded. It was pathetic to see such helplessness. But Esau stood firm on his lie and watched with smug satisfaction as they carted Jigger away.

That half a hog had cost Jigger two and a half years of hard labor on the penal farm. His will and spirit to love anyone else but his dear, sweet Louella was broken and they never returned to Esau's.

The tell tale signs of old age began to settle about them. The yard was neglected and overrun with chickens because the eggs were rarely gathered. Each year, fewer and fewer flowers came back. The birds had claimed the crabapple tree. The tin roof needed replacing, the bottom step had a bad case of rain rot, and the windows had started sagging. The once beautiful little house crumbled.   But they somehow managed to take care of each other inside their own sheltered world.

Chapter 6

The couple was in their nineties when some of Esau's grandchildren had got the papers to have Jigger committed to an old folk's home. Louella knew this was the doings of her people. Her father's dying wish had been living hell for her and Jigger. It seemed closer to reality now.

There was no crying or weeping this time. The will to fight for peace and unrequited love was gone. Seventy years was long enough. Their love and devotion to each other would sustain them to whatever destiny they faced.

She waited for them to come for her and like Jigger offered no resistance when they finally did. "Insane." That's what they said about her.

It never occurred to her that she would not end up at the same place they had taken her husband; but she was neither bitter nor disappointed when she didn't. She had outlived bitterness and learned to live with hurt.

For eighteen years more they suffered under circumstances over which they had no control. Jigger had two severe heart attacks and went through periods of almost total starvation, causing him to lose pounds that he could ill afford. Louella, as well, had refused food, and went down to skin and bones. Two strokes left her right side partially paralyzed and her eyes been to dim.

Yet, they both lived for love's sake.

Chapter 7

"Sonny," adventurous, and the baby boy of Harebell's youngest son, Henry, left home, heading north when he was in his late teens. There he met and married Ruby. The realization that they were raising their three boys without the benefit of knowing their full kin disturbed them and they decided to return home. Her people, ironically, lived only about forty miles from Sonny's hometown.

Sonny was certain Lou and Jigger had died by now and that their house could be lived in. As a young boy, he had seen his uncle beaten to death for speaking against the family for the treatment they gave Jigger and Lou. This had taught him to keep his thoughts about Lou and Jigger to himself. But he -was a man now and could face his feelings. He would cut the grass, fix the roof and windows, get his wife new curtains, maybe even raise a calf or two for the boys. The idea suited him fine.

His family was surprised to see him and welcomed them with open arms until he started asking about Lou, Jigger and the house. He felt the old tension, but ignored it, choosing to believe, instead; that maybe it was because some other family member wanted the house. Convinced he could not be persuaded to find another house, they told them Lou and Jigger had long been dead; but offered no help in fixing up the place. Sonny and his family had become the innocent victims of an endless circle of hate and deceit.

His first enthusiastic and necessary act was to

clear the path and yard to the house. It was certain that after all these years the property had become a den of varmints and snakes. Alone, he began the task of clearing the way to the house; hoping to finish before nightfall.

More devastating to him than any snake bite could have been was the letters he discovered in the mailbox. Most likely because the mailman refused to deliver any more mail after the box had become so completely overgrown with vines and grass. The postmark on the latest letter was eight months old. It was addressed: "Occupants, Route 3, Box 197." He couldn't make out the return address, but certainly felt entitled, not to mention compelled, to open it. "To kin or friends of Louella Johnson: Miss Louella is weak, dying, and needs comfort." Signed, Nurse Mary Watkins."

Sonny's hands began to tremble. His heart and mind raced. He folded the letter back, almost reverently, and put it in his pocket. He continued the task at hand with curious and renewed vengeance. "Just eight months ago - she could still be living...If they lied about Lou they must have lied about Jigger...Why did they lie...What now about the house?" All these perplexing thoughts filled his head; thoughts he knew he had to keep to himself.

Inside, the house was more livable than he had expected. It would be better than staying at a hotel or any of his relatives. He and his family moved in that night; and it was then he told Ruby what he had discovered.

A Sunday dawn, found Sonny heading out toward

old Highway 80. There were only two old folks homes that he knew of that were still standing. Blue Run, which was about twenty miles east of Sumpter and Willow Run, about the same distance west. When he reached the highway, he watched the traffic flow. It was heaviest going east - he would drive west.

The desolation of Willow Run Nursing Home was depressing. The grounds were barely kept and seemed as much a part of the woods as the woods itself. Vines even covered the small, one-story block building. If there were any windows, they were on the back side. The few cars parked around appeared as permanent as the building and undoubtedly belonged to the few employees. Anybody who would put someone in a place like this couldn't care enough to visit.

He found Mary Watkins in one of the dingy rooms, fussing over an old woman's hair, greasing her loose and withered scalp. "You might get some company today, Miss Lou," Sonny heard the fat friendly woman saying. She was unaware of his presence.

Sonny was dumfounded. He stood speechless, virtually reeling, overwhelmed by a love, by a compassion, by an anger he had never known before. He was certain there could be only one Miss Lou - his great aunt. It was impossible to believe he stood in the presence of blood over one hundred years old.

He got a grip on himself and fighting hard to control his anxiety and to hold back the tears, walked the few feet to the women and handed Miss Watkins the letter. "I've come to take her home," he said.

Miss Watkins paled beneath that silky, black skin; nearly fainting. He helped her to the bed where the three of them wept openly as Sonny recounted who he was and how he had come to be there.

Aunt Lou was feeble and weak; unable to walk, but ready and willing to go. And once again she left with nothing but the clothes she had on her back and the same old song in her heart.

They drove home slowly, savoring the purity of freedom and thoughts and moments they knew could never be relived. Aunt Lou was the first to break the silence. "You don't reckon you could go find Uncle Jigger for me, do you?" She had to chuckle. She had never been able to say "Uncle" Jigger.

Ruby and the boys were in overjoyed shock; and loved the idea of Aunt Lou living with them. It would obviously not be much longer, but they would cherish the time they did have with her. She was tired from the trip and had to be put to bed. She would be ready for her dinner of purple hull peas with okra, sweet potatoes and a good size hunk of corn-bread when she woke up.

Sonny and the boys were already making plans to go see about Jigger. It was no longer that unrealistic that he, too, could still be alive. Sleep didn't come easy that night for any of them, not even Aunt Lou. So they whiled away the hours listening to her tales and learning the only song she and Jigger ever sang.

Ruby stayed with Aunt Lou while Sonny and the boys made their journey to Blue Run. The seriousness of the trip was broken by five-year old Jonathan's simple, yet deserving stream of unending questions. "Daddy, if he doesn't have any teeth can he kiss her? What if he's got another girlfriend and doesn't want to come back? Maybe he'll be too fat to move.

All hope drained when it became obvious that the Blue Run Old Folks Home was unoccupied and out of business. Sonny pushed the car on ahead anyway, through the grass that had grown over the driveway and as close to the building as he could. He was so angry he wanted to ram the building. Even the children could not conceal their grief. Gregory, eleven, started crying. Jonathan, as usual, lightened the load, "Let's be like policemen and go peek inside. Maybe we'll find some secrets! It was agreed. They had nothing to lose.

Sonny cautioned them to watch the ground for snakes as they made their way around the building trying to find an open door or easy window. They had just rounded the corner when Thomas, the eldest, spotted a little boy running away from the building through the high-grassed open field. "Look" he shouted. There was no way they could catch him. He disappeared. What they were after was inside anyway.

They found the open door and went inside. It was a shambles; papers, old clothes and broken furniture, piled about the place. The stench of mildew and old urine filled the air. The only signs of life were the rats and roaches, which were in abundance. What could that little boy have been after?

The foursome walked abreast down the hall, peeping into each room. Sonny held Jonathan. "Daddy, do you think we oughta be looking at some of these papers?"   "Maybe we'll find his name on something-or something," Thomas asked.

"Well, I tell you what. We get down here to the end of the hall then we can work our way back. It shouldn't be hard to tell whether a man or a woman was in the room." Sonny answered.   Even he had begun to think like a detective.

They were not prepared for the shock they got as they passed the next to the last doorway.   The slumped figure in the chair before the window blended into the bleak austerity of the whole place.   Their eyes saw it, but they made a few steps beyond the door before the realization that they had seen a man hit them.

"Uncle Jigger!" they shouted in unison. They didn't know, but wanted so desperately for it to be him. He was so startled by the commotion his whole body trembled and the dish of, still warm, bread pudding crashed to the floor. Now they knew about the little boy they had seen running from the building.

He stared at them all without a word for so long they were beginning to believe they had made a mistake. "Who's calling Jigger?" he asked humbly. "Who's that calling me?"

He was weak, a little deaf and swelled; but it all came back to him as they sat clustered around, recounting and unravelling the past.   Sonny was especially careful to avoid direct questions about Louella. He wasn't sure Jigger could take knowing she was still alive. Jigger pulled out a dingy, ragged piece of what had once been sheet to blow his nose in an effort to conceal his happy tears.

They had to pry him from the chair which had become crusty with food and excrement, but it hardly mattered. When they got to the door, Uncle Jigger turned to take one last look at what had been his prison for so long. The silence was deafening. He reached into his pocket and pulled out his silver pocketwatch and hung it on the doorknob. "That boy was mighty good to me," he said reverently, and nodded his readiness to leave.

Little Jonathan was quiet going home.

Chapter 8

Aunt Lou's faith her Jigger was alive had never faltered. She was so confident he would be back with Sonny she even asked Ruby for some "smell good" and the chance to sit in the old rocker out back until he came,

"Honey," she began, reaching over tenderly patting Ruby's hand. "Let me tell you something. I am as old as you are young. Remember this. Love and honour your husband as you love and honour God. That each breath you draw be holy and one with the Master; that each thought and deed you do unto each other be one, for His glory. God promised what he put together, couldn't no man mess it up." She paused to let the tears flow, staring out into the sky. "As wrong as we was, we found peace in each other. The storms brewed all around us - all our life -and we ain't been shook loose yet. But the storm is passing over... praise the Lord. "Jigger Lives!" From her heart, the words flowed and the burden seemed to lift with each breath she took.

Ruby wanted to leave, but was held spellbound as Aunt Lou continued.

"You see, most things the good Lord just lets be. But some things He reaches out and touches. And that's the way He did us. We didn't intend this love, Jigger and me. It just happened. But he reached out His mighty hand and plucked out me and Jigger, just like he done plucked you and Sonny." she said smiling, looking at Ruby. "And he drew us up close to his bosom and blew his breath on us. And then He put us back on this ol' dried up earth and said 'Love.'." She paused a long time. "It wasn't nothin' else for us to do but obey. Honey, we didn't sing that song for nothin.' That was our song, and now it's got to be yours." She went off to sleep singing it within, waiting for Jigger.

Ruby sat thoughtfully, not minding the tears that trickled as she weighed the words Aunt Lou had left her. They would last her a lifetime. The silence was broken by the car coming up the drive. She knew it was Sonny and the boys. With care, she eased out the chair and off the porch then ran around the front to meet them to motion them quiet.

It took Uncle Jigger a while to realize that he was home. Nonetheless, he never stopped asking for his Louella. Ruby and Sonny wanted to clean him up a bit before taking him out on the porch to be with Aunt Lou, but he was too distraught to prolong the suspense any longer. He, too, knew she was alive.

Ruby woke Aunt Lou gently to tell her they had found Uncle Jigger while Thomas and Sonny carried him through the house out back and set him in the old rocker close to Aunt Lou.

The moment was tender. They looked at each other and wept unashamedly. "These are our children, Jigger," Aunt Lou said.

Sonny and the boys, along with their mother, went around to the front porch to give Aunt Lou and Uncle Jigger privacy. Jonathan had to tell Mama all about it; leaving no stone unturned. They talked about the additional room they would need to build on. Greg wanted to fatten them up so they would be strong enough again to get around by themselves. They had all sorts of plans. Sonny, in the back of his mind was wondering how he was going to deal with his family. Right then, however, he was wondering about dinner. "What you got for dinner, Mama?" he asked affectionately, smacking his wife on her rear.

"Chicken and dumplings, sugar," she answered sweetly, throwing her arms around his neck. The boys liked this. They had learned to ask for favors during affectionate moments like these; but this day was special. It belonged to Lou and Jigger.

"Are you and Daddy gonna live as long as Aunt Lou and Uncle Jigger?" Jonathan asked, squeezing between them.

"Well, let's hope so," they said as they were getting up and heading into the house.

"Let's go fix them a plate of dumplings," Sonny said, squeezing Thomas' shoulder. "We'll let them eat on the porch, alone."

Ruby fixed two plates, put them on TV trays and she and Sonny carried them their dinner. They were holding hands and smiling. They had just died.

Chapter 9

As Mama Rosie wiped tears from her eyes I could remember wondering why she was crying. It wasn't until I was much older that I realized this wasn't just a story she had made up, or some folklore that had been handed down through the years but; it was in fact her family story. The lady the whole town had become accustomed to calling Mama Rosie was none other than Ruby Johnson, Sonny's wife. Not many people knew her story or her real name. Not many people knew the history of the land she lived on, or quite understood why she tended this land with so much care for all these years. The only common knowledge was that she had a husband and he died many years ago. I would often wonder why she spent all these years alone; now I knew the reason. Mama Rosie was as tough as nails and ten times wiser and stronger than any man I had ever known. Seeing her shed a tear was something I thought impossible, so those tears carved a path deep into my soul. When I raised myself off of Mama Rosie's lap that day, she whispered in my ear, "I've never told that story to anyone son, keep it in your heart, and no matter how old you get, remember one thing...True love is inseparable and never dies."

Helping Mama Rosie in her garden later that afternoon took on a totally different meaning to me somehow. "Come over here boy!" she shouted to me. As I drew closer she said "walk with me for awhile." We made our way past the ripe watermelons and the green peppers whose scent was so vibrant you could almost taste them. We passed the stone well which was not only the life source of her garden but to all of us who drank of its waters. And then we headed down this narrow path covered with leaves and sticks and rocks. "We're here" she said, as she pointed to that old oak tree that I would often see Squala grunting at. "That's where we buried them" she exclaimed fighting back tears.

Not even death could keep Lou and Jigger apart.

Me my mother and brother

Me and my older brother Ken Childress

My Mother Marilyn Edith Childress(1947-1998)

Mama Rosie

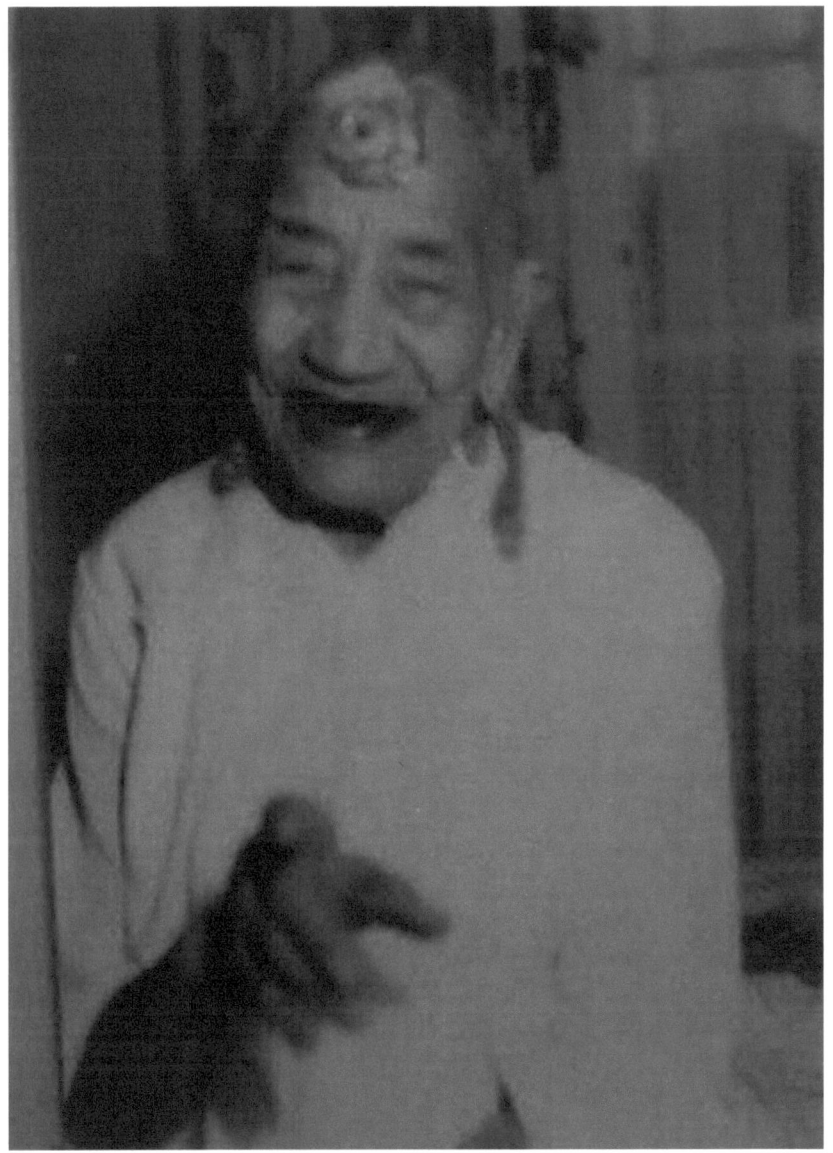

Squala

www.ingramcontent.com/pod-product-compliance
Lightning Source LLC
Chambersburg PA
CBHW041729240626
47171CB00001B/6